A GIFTED LIFE

SATHIYA NARAYANAN

To my beloved mother who taught me to read and write. Love you till my last breath and beat.

Contents

Acknowledgements   *vii*

Prologue   *ix*

    1. Whispers Of The Past   1

    2. The Gifted Curse   5

    3. Silent Revelations   12

Epilogue   15

Acknowledgements

I am deeply grateful to my parents for their unwavering support and encouragement throughout this journey.

To my friends, thank you for your constant inspiration and for always being there to cheer me on.

Your love and belief in me have been my greatest strength.!

Prologue

"I feel nothing," Surya confessed.

"Are you sure, no pain?" the Doctor looked concerned.

"Thanks for the concern Doctor, but still nothing," Surya said sarcastically.

But in reality, the pain was excruciating, and felt like he was being punctured by thousands of needles even though he had just been injected by only one.

"You're a strong boy, Surya. I can guarantee you that," Doctor assured him with an encouraging smile.

Surya responded with a nod and a fake smile. He knew that his father would come to know if he resists the treatment. It was not the first time he got forced into this "Regular check-up" and it definitely won't be the last time but he never knew the real reason behind it. As his father was not present for today's session, Surya tried to push his luck.

"Am I alright, Doctor??" Surya asked innocently.

Poor boy worried about the....

Then came the absolute silence. Surya was not able to understand. Typically he roams around the Doctor's gullible mind but today he felt a sudden blockade on infiltering. Surya looked at the Doctor curiously. There it was quite obvious on the Doctor's face that he was terrified of him. Surya cursed his father for this. It should have been his father's doing as they both were best mates from the school.

"There's nothing wrong with you kid," the Doctor's voice quivered but he tried to stay calm.

Surya understood that nothing could be extracted from him and wondered how could someone block him intentionally. He could ask his mother though but she probably would not answer.

As for his mother, he would rather ignore that topic because there was nothing to tell. Let's just say, she was not in the picture for the most part. He only knew that it didn't work out between his parents but he solemnly blames his father for that matter. It was just not easy to live and cope with such a person as his father. The only good thing he could think of his father was that he never laid a hand on him which was not surprising as his father never really expressed anything to him. Surya always wondered how could someone even live without emotions and expressions at all. There would be no laughter, no sadness, no anger or fear, no guilt or regret, no shame or sympathy, an absolute nothingness on his stern unblinking father's face. It just feels so weird.

Surya thanked the Doctor and collected the medicines he had prescribed. His father's driver was waiting for him in the parking lot. He hated his father for keeping him under watch at all times.

He came straight back to his house, a two-story moderate structure on the outskirts of Bangalore. They had an old basement where they used to store old stuff of his father and their ancestor's long-lost belongings. Surya cleared some space in the middle of the basement with a low light bulb hanging barely from the ceiling. It became his only place to find solace despite the nauseating experience he had down here.

Surya eyed the dairy he found a few days back among the junk in a tray of old books. It gave away a nasty rusted smell and sent a lot of fine dust particles along with it. He was also curious about the handwritten notes inside the dairy in which most of the writings were faded and ruined by decades of unruly maintenance. He found that it belonged to his father, and wondered how a person like him could ever maintain a daily journal in his early teens.

It was a quarter to six in the evening and he knew it would be another two hours before his father made it home. Surya lethargically flipped through the pages and finally stopped at the journal's last entry. He just wanted to laugh out loud about what his emotionless father had written all those years ago.

Date: 22/01/95

My dear reader,

Tell me how can a gift become a curse?....

I have always had this question, right from the moment my uncle asked me this. If you could ask my mother, her simple reply would be, "If this is what God wishes, then it shall be". But she would not, as she is no more. It's been a year since her death and I'm still mourning her loss. She would always say whenever someone passes away that they are in a better place right now.

I very much doubt that in fact I completely contradict her saying. How could God alone wish for anything he likes and take everything he wants?

My mother would call it "God's Will" but I prefer "God's Dictatorship". She often punishes me for that.

Once I read about this Tsunami caused by an earthquake that wiped out nearly 60,000 people. I asked my mother about this incident in front of her religious study group. She answered with the same old phrase "God's Will" with a grim face. And I corrected her proudly saying "If killing that many people is God's Will, then either he is not as powerful as you say or he is not as kind and good as you praise".

Well, that was all it took for her to pinch my ear till she left me with a permanent scar on my earlobe. But it is nothing compared to the scar that she left behind in my heart. I know I sound dramatic and poetic. All thanks to her for making me a reading person after all. Actually, I'm not a literature person but very much into stories and stuff and that was how my mother told me to experiment with certain books which turned out pretty good. And that was also how I moved into philosophical and "Questioning God" concepts.

But none of those things helped me to conclude the question I have. Every different topic and concept drives me into a different reality of possibilities. My uncle said the question has no specific answer if you search for it but it was what it is and it has always been and it always will be. He also said this gift has been there for generations after generations. For each one it had various effects he said, in some generations, the one who possesses that gift prospers more, and in another, they suffer more. Few have controlled and mastered it with ease and some have been driven mad because of it.

And in his case, it was my mother who got the gift from their family. She was quite the prodigy that everyone thought she could handle until she could not. Everyone from my mother's side blamed me because they firmly believed one should not give birth at their prime time. I guess they never really figured out how it works and it was all part of legends and myths. Anyway, I finally learned why my family despised me after all this time.

But I never learned what had happened to her medically. All my father told me was that she had skin cancer and it got worse in a couple of years. She was actually fine undergoing treatment and recovering gradually and all of a sudden something happened. No doctor was able to explain what went wrong in her case. I still hear her last words to me, "It was...It was never a gift...I'm so sorry" with tears rolling down her cheeks.

My headache is getting much worse day by day as I was diagnosed with Hyperacusis. It generally is the increased sensitivity to sound and a low tolerance for environmental noise. It got worse during my Mother's funeral, where I ended up with my ears bleeding and finally fainting.

The doctors have said that the only solution is partial lobotomy. But as a post-surgical aftereffect, I may suffer from extreme pain or may not feel any emotions at all.

So probably I am not sure whether I will be able to continue journaling in the future. If so I would like to apologize to a whole lot of people but I hope I did not disappoint you who have come all the way to put up with my stupid journaling.

ONE

WHISPERS OF THE PAST

Surya was confused and not sure about what was going on. There was too much information about his father running through his head and it was a lot to process. But something seemed familiar about it and he just could not piece the puzzle. Both intrigued and a little nervous, he went all the way to the front to read the first-ever entry.

Date: 08/05/94

My dear reader,

I just want to appreciate whoever is eager to read this. I do not want to go through all of my personal details since I have already filled it on the front page of this diary.

And I'm 14 by the way.

So basically I'm not a journaling person who pens down everything that happens day after day. Though I have been advised by many to do so, I never had the urge to write it down until today.

I would have laughed my heart out if someone had told me that today would be the day of all the days I would be putting myself down to write my journal. Because today is the last day of my annual board exams and usually right after which I have never stayed home but roamed and played all around the town till I have to drag myself to my home in exhaustion. But an exception happened today. Something extraordinary occurred during my exam.

My whole family is buzzing around the room, curious about what I'm doing on a night like this. Everyone was surprised except for my mother when I yelled at them that I needed privacy since I was writing my journal. She looked at me with a calm and stern face and seemed both happy and sad for me. It seems weird to have her look at me like that. As a matter of fact, everything seems weird at this point.

Okay... back to the topic. As usual, it was a science exam that always came at last. It was like some grand finale of a random reality show. The questions were very tough or I can say it will be for those who had never gone through the book. The way I usually work was to ignore all these good-for-nothing unit tests and put everything into the final exams to pass that term. My mother found out my pattern of this strategy and scolded me for such behavior. I reassured her that nothing bad would happen and everything was under control. She cursed me in return that one day I have to pay for all my sins. Well, finally today is the day it looks like all my sins have caught up with me.

Let me explain... As usual, a week back, I neglected all the unit test worries and was playing cricket with my friends carefree. And that was when while trying to take an impossible catch, my little finger got fractured. In a way of making matters worse, it was the finger of my writing hand and the annual exams were getting nearer. My mother's caring yet "I told you" eyes burned me with guilt and regret. That was when I realized no matter how much effort I put into learning things it would be a waste of time if I'm not able to write it on the answer sheet.

Despite all odds, I was able to finish the rest of the exams with a slight hope of scoring passing marks. But it all comes down to this exam which I knew for sure would cause a wreck in my life. I simply had no hope for today and I was going through all the worst possibilities and disastrous outcomes like no sports, no late-night outings, no pocket money, no TV and movies, literally nothing.

Even during the middle of the exam, I was considering these and was awaiting the inevitable until that exact moment when I heard the fragments of answers for the question Ohm's law. I searched around frantically, looking for the dead guy who blurted the "precious" answer out loud. But to my disappointment, no one was there. The invigilator glared at me and made a gesture to say, "Do it next time and you're doomed.!".

Then I sunken back into my hole and was perplexed about the incident, it felt both weird and abnormal.

'Ohm's Law states that.... the relationship between... Electric current and potential difference...' Once again I heard the faint but staggering voice, moving slowly throughout the hall but no one seemed to notice it.

At the moment, I just followed my instinct and kept on scribbling down the words, the voice had spoken. I knew I was not able to catch up with the voice's speed due to my injury and missed a lot of things in between but I just did not care.!!

It was during that afternoon post-lunch when we all were so eager to get out of school and enjoy our weekend holidays, I heard that voice again. At least this time I confirmed that I was not dreaming before. I was not able to follow it since the whole class was in a whole different vibe. I concentrated a bit harder on it and eventually tracked it down. It was like following a faint but pleasant smell amid chaos. It was Harish, after all, our class topper the one who received the Exceptional

Student Award. Everyone was teasing and bullying him for still studying even though the exams were over. He didn't mind them but got frustrated for disturbing his 'Reading Ritual'. It was not visible on his face but I could sense it as if I could read his mind. An evil smile and more of an evil plan crept into my head.

TWO

THE GIFTED CURSE

Surya skimmed through the rotten yellow pages to read the next entry and all that followed were lost to the ages. But in the middle, he found an entry legible enough to read.

Date: 13/08/94

Dear Reader,

I sincerely apologize because I know it has been quite some time since my last entry. I apologize for keeping you guys away from my extraordinary journey of a gifted life.

Yes, I could proudly say it is a gifted life whereas my mother used to preach that "Every life is a gifted one..!". I know it is simply not possible to have a natural conversation with her. So, to explain my "Gifted Life", I have to narrate the details precisely and not exaggerate things just to boast of my superhuman potential, mind you.

For the first few days, it was like floating in a dream mesmerized by the power of my mind and whatever it is capable of. It was like giving Charles Xavier's "Cerebro" from the X-Men comics to a desperate kid in the world. I nearly went crazy when I tried to use more of it the other day. I know, I may sound like a crazy comic superhero who typically after finding out their superhuman power would not be able to control it at first but gradually master it.

I could agree with that. Right after fiddling around with Harish for some days and understanding the strategy of how he stores and recollects his memories, I tried to read others' minds but it didn't do any good. I heard static-like noise around most of them but sometimes was able to hear some mumbling and whispering of people in their minds but it was hard to pinpoint them. It took me several days to figure it out and I don't intend to bore you with that. Let's just say that it was like tuning the frequency on the radio to find the right channel.

Some people's minds are easy to manipulate if they feel inferior to others so I can go through their minds and look into all the thoughts they have collected and stored as if watching a movie by picking whatever there is in their whole collection of memories. Even a long-lost memory can be brought into the picture but most of them would be a traumatic incident or a less important one. In either case, the vision is going to be blurry and vague as it becomes a faded memory. They won't understand anything on why they are having the thoughts they have at the moment. Those people would be completely clueless and feel bad about themselves for getting such thoughts. Sometimes I feel pity for them.

On the other hand, people with a strong mindset tend to resist an outside force and many would suffer from severe headaches and migraines. It was like running a mini car through the wall. It causes damage but the wall won't budge until it's not strong enough to hold. I followed a systematic plan and categorized people into majors and miners who could resist my power and those who could not. In this way, I was able to get to people beyond my class and neighbors.

In fact, I tried to do some research on my superpower with the help of a "Library Friend" who introduced me to some supernatural terms like 'Telekinesis' and 'Telepathy'. He explained that studies and scientific research are being conducted to prove such psychic abilities but have never received any clear evidence of their existence.

I literally felt like Charles Xavier with silly intentions and stupid ideas. And all that came to a breaking point where it was not supposed to end that way but it became inevitable.

It was during the middle of term exams that I learned about about this competition. It was a school-level quiz tournament. Usually, I don't mind these dumb competitions as I considered these exclusively for the nerds but since I started to perform well in my academics(you-know-how), I decided to excel in this one. All you need is a partner to participate in the prelims and my initial approach was to pair up with Harish because obviously, he is going to outperform everyone else. But then later I saw Farzana consumed deep in her thoughts on whom to partner up with. She was really so confused and felt insecure about others but she never showed any of this on her beautiful face as she rejected as many suitors just to find the right one. Mind you, beautiful in the sense of the abundant knowledge that resides in her. And I know very well who would fit right in.

I became her partner just by speaking the right words that she wanted to hear. The baffled murmurs and the shocking whispers from everyone were like honey to my ears. No one could barely believe how I landed with Farzana despite all the odds. I could sense the scorching jealousy and anger toward me radiating from all directions and I just bathed calmly in their emotions. But what surprised me is that she never bothered to have a second thought about her decision to go with me regardless of her annoying friends constantly influencing her mind by saying ill of me.

I must honestly admit some of them are painfully true but that does not make me a bad person. She also mentioned on the day before the competition that she simply wanted someone to accompany her and she would do the rest and take care of the winning. I could tell that she wasn't lying but also she didn't tell the entire truth because the truth is, she liked having me on the team. The irony is, that she could hide all these feelings from her face and to all others but not from me.

At last, the day came when no one expected my arrival. I let her do all the necessary registration process by pulling a little act before everyone that I don't even know how to fill out all these application forms. That was more than enough for my competitors to conclude that I'm a dim-witted person and pose no threat to any of them. I intentionally fooled them all including Farz who no longer considered me suitable for her and the team.

Good to know, because when someone starts from zero and has nothing to lose, nobody wants to mess with them. I know that I sound so cool but I can't help it. Apologies..!!

It started with the prelims. There were around 50 pairs of teams swarming the entire auditorium along with several audiences flanking them. As it was a knockout round, most of the teams were supposed to be filtered, leaving only 10 of them for the next round. And on the next one, to match my naive stupid demeanor, I purposely shouted absolute and wrong answers and lost some points at the cost of Farz's distaste.

By putting the emotions out of her mind, she calmly explained certain things and firmly warned me not to press the buzzer until and unless I discussed the answer with her. She was really stunned by my behavior and started to believe that I was really not capable of pulling this off. I suddenly felt bad for myself and promised her secretly that I would make things right.

Anyway, somehow we managed and qualified for the final round through Farz's capability. But I could tell that she was not ready for what was coming and she had a nagging sensation that things won't go right from now on. Alright, it was time to step up.

By the time the final round started, the crowd seemed to multiply immensely and occupied most of the spaces in the auditorium. I could feel the huge traffic of thoughts running through my mind wildly which made me a little dizzy. It was really hard to concentrate on Farz's thoughts even though she was right beside me.

That was when I realized that in a crowded situation if I had to access the right person's mind sometimes I have to look at them to concentrate. I mean literally. Like pointing the remote control towards the TV in order to get the right channel.

So back in the game, the Quiz Master was explaining the rules for the final round to the contestants but nothing went inside for me. We had a little break of refreshments before starting and in the meantime, Farz explained it to me.

Each team will have 3 sets of questions and each carries 1 point whereas if answered wrongly it will be -1. In the end, we will also have one final buzzer question that the team that presses the buzzer first can answer. If answered correctly 10 whole points will be given and if not -10. The catch was that once it was pressed you had to answer it. It was like a Do or Die question. You will lose definitely if your answer is wrong no matter whatever points you gained from the previous questions.

During the 1ˢᵗ set of questions, Roshan and Harish's team answered correctly and when it was our turn, I could see that Farz was panicking and that was when I pounced back with the right answer. Most of the crowd was stunned by my performance as no one expected it from me. Even Farz seemed surprised. And for the second answer, everyone in the audience gasped in shock. Farz smiled and felt stupid for doubting me. Strong emotions welled up in me but I wanted to save them for later.

But the Quiz Master noticed something fishy. I could tell by his look. The rest of the teams answered all three correctly and by the time when I was supposed to answer, the Master stopped and asked me to look at him to answer. I sensed satisfaction from him as I struggled with this one. It was really hard for me to concentrate without looking. Finally, I whispered to Farz to pass this question so that we would not lose a point. I cursed the Master for figuring it out, he didn't get why I was not able to answer but somehow knew I was cheating.

The final set with the buzzer was the worst. Not only were we the team with the least points but we were also the last team to press the buzzer. Rohan's team who had already scored a point from me was struggling to find an answer and eventually passed the question to defend his lead in the scoreboard and frantically praying for us to fail. I could see Harish squeeze and rack his brain for an answer but none came. He too then gave up at the end so that at least they could be the runner-up.

At last, it all came down to me. I could surely tell Farz was convinced that they could never win this one and I want to prove her wrong. Very badly though.

Once again the Master had locked his small suspicious eyes on me, and that was when I decided to try him out.

Left with no other choice, I pursued the inevitable one. As I have said before, people like this Master who I assume as Majors were quite complicated. The wall he posed against me was strong enough to hold. I knew that it can withstand the dashing of a car, so I tried to smash it with a truck this time. I could sense the vibration of his walls through my head but still, it stood intact.

So I step down a lot harder on it. And that was when I lost control of it.

Everything went crazy right after that. Everyone started screaming in a high-pitched tone and looked wild as if they were all turning into a werewolf or something under a full moon. Some were holding their heads in a tight grip like it was going to explode and some were scratching others and themselves ferociously while crying at the top of their lungs. And very few people... I would strongly suggest that this would be really disturbing... I'm still getting nightmares even after several weeks of agony.

Very few people started to tremble all over and their eyes got rolled back, showing only the whites where the supposed pupil had to be and when I thought this couldn't be much weirder, they started to lift off the ground, floating in the bare air with blood spilling out of their white eyes and suddenly it all looked like demonic possession.

My vision started to blur gradually and I was kind of glad as I could no longer able to witness the catastrophe. Hot blood trickled down from my left nostril and I could feel the metallic taste in my mouth. Of all this trouble, the severe migraine was the worst. It struck me like a solid force, my legs gave way as I hit the ground and my body started to twitch uncontrollably. The pain felt very alien as if my brain was being penetrated with a thousand needles. The last thing I remember before I blacked out was that the Master pointed at me and stuttered "E.. Ev.. Evvilll...".

THREE

SILENT REVELATIONS

Date: 08/12/94

And as you know now this was the reason that I was away for a while. I had been hospitalized and undergone various tests and scanning before I got discharged 10 days back.

The school has been closed since that day and informed there is a police investigation going on what exactly happened, so until further notice the school has been temporarily shut down.

During the hospital stay, my mother hasn't left my side for a whole week. It was not a surprising thing as most mothers tend to do. But we came to a certain understanding along the way. First of all, she was aware of the entire activity since it started and merely waited for the triggering point to calm me down.

She knew that I would never listen even if she tried to hammer me with absolute warnings. She also admitted that she doesn't have any strength to match me right now. Despite all the commotion that I made the previous week, she was very kind to me which was not her usual self.

"Look at me.." she whispered. It was too bright that morning and my eyes welled up with tears as I tried squinting at her. I was searching her face for any expression that she wanted me to see.

"Look at me.." she repeated. But this time she surprised me. Her face had the most neutral expression which she only gives when she wants my utmost serious attention. It was her mouth, it didn't even move or make a sound. It was just as passive and calm and composed as it could be. And that was when I realized that she was not speaking for the entire time.

I felt her eyes piercing through me like a fine needle with nothing but a slight prickle. Normally, when I do this to a person I can sense the amount of pain they go through as I have said before like driving a mini-van into a wall. The sturdiness of the wall depends on each individual's capability and sheer will. Despite how feeble I seemed during those hospital stays I still knew that I had enough strength in me to defend myself. But what I experienced was the complete opposite.

She broke through my defense wall not with a heavy truck or anything but just with a tiny needle. I lay there in shock, trying to remember what was I supposed to do as she was going through my memories seamlessly. She had done with me before I had time to think of a counter strategy to resist. She sighed heavily and gave a slow nod when she withdrew from me.

In returning the favor, I made a blunt mistake. I rushed into her mind with such brute force, that I did not even think to notice that her defense wall was more vulnerable than mine. I refused to mind her mere attempts to hold me back. And when I came back, my heart was broken. What I saw in there, scared me to death. Part of me wanted this to be a false memory and left behind but deep down I knew it was a bitter reality. She was not going to survive any longer. The thought of realizing that this may be my final moment with her, made me shiver to my bones. Tears flowed down as I gasped for breath.

Embarrassed, I turned away facing her. She coughed lightly, struggling to maintain her posture. And despite all my wrongdoings, she forgave me. Her preaching still ringing in my ears on how one should worship the Almighty on such hard occasions. On how it was his will to take those he likes and all the stuff associated with that.

She said it is hereditary and it has to stop along with her. There is a way she hesitated, that could prevent me from this chaos.

I did not object to her like I always did. I complied with a heavy heart because I did not want to argue during what might be my precious moments with her. Tears clouded my sight and slowly I faded into the darkness as I wished I had said everything I wanted to say. I just wished I had more time.

Epilogue

Surya tried to read more but met with a dead end as there were no more entries that were legible to read. It became much harder to believe it. He never for once considered his father as a doable person. His mind began to piece together as realization hit him like lightning.

An inevitable silence followed. The picture he drew of his father in his mind as a cruel, self-centered, selfish, and emotionless man slowly faded into the shadows. Instead, he caught glimpses of his father with a stern face, always being polite, never raising his voice or hand, and never showing any anger in his eyes.

Surya always assumed that his father just simply lacked feelings for anyone and that was why his mother had left them. Unfortunately, he never came to know about the surgery that his father had and the effects it had on him. He did some research on Google for Partial Lobotomy and found that such surgeries are done only in rare conditions who are suffering from extreme pain in their head. As a post-surgical after-effect, one may suffer from severe pain or may not feel any emotions at all.

Things started to be clearer than ever and began to fall into place. His father knew he had those abilities right from the start and eventually, it would come down to this. He knew that the cycle never stops and that history repeats itself. But he wants to fight it otherwise his son's life will be doomed just like his.That should be the reason why his father moved to a place where you get to meet very few people compared to a bustling city. The fewer people you talk to, the lesser the problem arises.

Footsteps came from the above. Surya rushed and hid the dairy under the floorboard. His father stood at the bottom of the stairs and looked at him. It was then he noticed that his father had warm eyes but it was just his face that lacked emotions. Dust swirled between them. Surya muffled a cough to fill the silence.

Guilt consumed his heart as bitter memories of him cursing his father for losing his mother, and despised his emotionless behavior. Even humiliated him publicly for being dumb and worthless. He had wished him to be dead.

Tears welled up and soaked his eyes which he desperately tried to suppress. Words stuck in his throat and nothing came to his mind.

"I'm sorry..." Surya mumbled but it did not reach his lips.

"You don't have to..!" his father whispered back.